RHYME TIME

Little Miss Muffet

& OTHER RHYMES

Illustrated by

Kareen Taylorson

Purnell

Little
Miss Muffet

Little Miss Muffet,
Sat on a tuffet,
Eating her curds and whey.
Along came a spider,
Who sat down beside her,
And frightened Miss Muffet away.

Boys and girls,
come out to play

Boys and girls, come out to play,
The moon doth shine as bright as day,
Leave your supper, and leave your sleep,
And come with your playfellows into the street.

Come with a whoop, come with a call,
Come with a good will, or come not at all.
Up the ladder and down the wall,
A halfpenny loaf will serve us all.
You find milk, and I'll find flour,
And we'll have pudding in half an hour.

The Queen of Hearts

The Queen of Hearts
She made some tarts,
All on a summer's day;
The Knave of Hearts
He stole those tarts,
And took them clean away.

The King of Hearts
Called for the tarts,
And beat the Knave full sore;
The Knave of Hearts
Brought back the tarts,
And vowed he'd steal no more.

Jack and Jill

Jack and Jill went up the hill
To fetch a pail of water;
Jack fell down and broke his crown
And Jill came tumbling after.

Little Jack Horner

Little Jack Horner,
Sat in a corner,
Eating a Christmas pie.
He put in his thumb,
And pulled out a plum,
And said "What a good boy am I"

If...

If all the world were apple pie,
And all the seas were ink,
And all the trees were bread and cheese
What should we have for drink?

Monday's child

Monday's child is fair of face,
Tuesday's child is full of grace,
Wednesday's child is full of woe,
Thursday's child has far to go,

Friday's child is loving and giving,
Saturday's child works hard for a living,
But the child that is born on the Sabbath day
Is bonny and blithe, and good and gay.

There was an old woman who lived in a shoe

There was an old woman who lived in a shoe,
She had so many children she didn't know what to do.
She gave them some broth without any bread;
She whipped them all soundly and put them to bed.

For
every evil

For every evil under the sun,
There is a remedy, or there is none.
If there be one, try and find it;
If there be none, never mind it.

There was a little girl

There was a little girl, and she had a little curl
Right in the middle of her forehead;
When she was good she was very, very good,
But when she was bad she was horrid.

Georgie Porgie

Georgie Porgie, pudding and pie,
Kissed the girls and made them cry;
When the boys came out to play,
Georgie Porgie ran away.

Jack Sprat

Jack Sprat could eat no fat,
His wife could eat no lean,
And so, between them both, you see,
They licked the platter clean.

Twinkle, twinkle, little star

Twinkle, twinkle, little star,
How I wonder what you are!
Up above the moon so high,
Like a diamond in the sky.

Hush-a-bye, baby

Hush-a-bye, baby, on the tree top,
When the wind blows, the cradle will rock;
When the bough breaks, the cradle will fall,
Down will come baby, cradle and all.

The End

A PURNELL BOOK

First published in Great Britain in 1987 by
Macdonald and Co (Publishers) Ltd,
London & Sydney
A BPCC plc company

Devised and produced by Templar Publishing Ltd,
107 High Street, Dorking, Surrey RH4 1QA

Copyright © 1987 by Templar Publishing Ltd
Illustrations copyright © 1987 by Templar Publishing Ltd

Designed by Mick McCarthy
Colour separations by Positive Colour Ltd, Maldon, Essex
Printed in Great Britain by Purnell Book Production Ltd,
Member of the BPCC Group

Macdonald and Co (Publishers) Ltd,
Greater London House, Hampstead Road, London NW1 7QX

British Library Cataloguing in Publication Data
Rhyme time
    Little Miss Muffet and other rhymes.
    1. Nursery rhymes, English
    I. Taylorson, Kareen
    398'.8   PZ8.3

ISBN 0-361-07662-2